DANCE OF SOUNDS

DANCE OF SOUNDS

DEJAN STOJANOVIĆ

New Avenue Books

New Avenue Books

First Edition

Library of Congress Control Number: 2025934783

ISBN-13: 9781966571148

NOTE TO THIS EDITION

The poems in this collection are part of a series titled *The Embrace of Light and Darkness,* marking their first publication in book form. The collection includes poems originally written in English between 2005 and 2010.

D. S.

Contents

FORGOTTEN HOME

FORGOTTEN HOME

My feelings are too loud for words
And too shy for the world.
See the Light and have a dream
In your hidden garden.
No need for words.

The words are but shadows
Of stories never told,
Shining from distant kingdoms,
Reminding you of a forgotten home.

Light rays will tell you the story.
There is another alphabet
Whispering from every leaf,
Singing from every river,
Shimmering from every sky.

BEING LATE

The simplicity and ease of movement
Of heavenly bodies stem from precision.
The Sun is never late to rise upon the Earth,
The Moon is never late to cause the tides,
The Earth is never late to greet the Sun and the Moon.
Thus, accidents are not accidents,
But precise arrivals at the wrong-right time.
Love is seldom simple.
Too often, feelings arrive too soon,
Waiting for thoughts that often come too late.
I, too, wanted to be simple and precise,
Like the Sun, the Moon, and the Earth,
But the Earth has been booked billions of years in advance,
Designed to meet all desires, all arrivals,
All sunrises, all sunsets, and all departures,
So I will have to be a little bit late.

TASK OF A POET

To hear never-heard sounds,

To see never-seen colors and shapes,

To try to understand the imperceptible

Power pervading the world;

To fly and find pure, ethereal substances

Beyond material form,

Yet part of the invisible essence that infuses reality.

To hear the soul of another and whisper to them;

To be a lantern in the darkness

Or an umbrella on a stormy day;

To feel much more deeply than to know.

To be the eyes of an eagle, the slope of a mountain;

To be a wave attuned to the pull of the Moon;

To be a tree that remembers the stories of its leaves;

To be an unnoticed pedestrian on the streets

Of bustling cities, observing and reflecting.

To be a smile on a woman's face

And shine in her memory

As a moment saved without planning.

SOUNDS OF IMAGINATION

I imagined I was a mountain,
Then I became a cloud over that mountain.
Lightning and thunder pummeled the mountain,
Pierced the heart of the Earth,
Becoming lava and exploding as a volcano.

I imagined I was a star,
Light traveling into space.
Then I grew as a tree,
With leaves of galaxies eating the light,
Becoming the angel of life and the bearer of light.

I imagined I was a black hole,
Flying through myself and swallowing myself,
While eating others to consume the abyss of energy.
But still, holding the whole galaxy in order,
Keeping billions of stars circling me.

I imagined I was God for a millisecond
And became speechless for a long time.

BIG MINIATURE

To transform a grimace into a sound
Sounds impossible, yet it is possible
To transform a vision into music,
Breaking free from an enslaved personality
To become impersonal by transforming
Into sand, water, or light,
To feel the air and breathe it in
By becoming the air, a bird,
The first cell, the first man,
A wandering comet, a dying star,
A newborn cluster of stars
And hear the melody of galaxies,
Experience the Love of black stars,
The hellish or heavenly nature of quasars,
Be in everything and come back
To a minuscule particle of personality
To discover how magnificent all of this is.

DANCING OF SOUNDS

There is a moonlight note
In the *Moonlight Sonata;*
There is a thunderous note
In an angry sky.

Sound, unbound by nature,
Is confined by art.
There is no competition between
A nightingale and a violin.

Nature rewards and punishes
In unpredictable ways;
Art is apotheosis;
Often, the complaint of beauty.

Nature is an outcry,
Unpolished truth;
The art—a euphemism—
Tamed wilderness.

SILENCE IS THE UNIVERSAL LIBRARY

Is there ever a true moment of silence?
Such a moment cannot exist
Unless we return
To the world before its creation.

Since nothing is absolute
There is no absolute silence—
Only the appearance
Of temporary peace.

Since real silence does not exist,
Silence encompasses all sounds,
All words, all languages,
All knowledge, and all memory.

Everything is contained within this library
In the Brain of the Universe—
Its source of inexhaustible energy,
The Library of Silence.

POSSIBILITY

Everything may seem impossible
Yet everything can also appear possible.
Possible impossibilities arise
From seemingly impossible possibilities,
Or perhaps impossible possibilities
Blossom from the impossibly possible.

A possibility is largely a matter of attitude,
A choice to select
From the realm of impossible options,
When one promising opportunity
Turns into a viable solution.

UNDERSTANDING

Is it possible to understand the impossible?

Based on the law of probability,

Everything is possible

Because the sheer existence of possibility

Confirms the existence of impossibility.

To understand the possible

Means to grasp the impossible.

SIMPLICITY

The most complicated skill
Is to be simple.

To say more while saying less
Is the secret of being simple.

To not say all that can be said
Is the secret of discipline and economy.

To leave out beautiful sunsets
Is the secret of good taste.

To hide feelings when you are near crying
Is the secret of dignity.

To cut and tighten sentences
Is the secret of mastery.

To keep the air fresh among words
Is the secret of verbal cleanliness.

To write good poems
Is the secret of brevity.

To go against the grain
Is the secret of bravery.

To risk life to save a smile on the face of a woman or a child
Is the secret of chivalry.

To go where no one else has ever gone before
Is the secret of heroism.

To expect to be kissed having bad breath
Is the secret of a fool.

Words rich in meaning
Can be cheap in sound effects.

QUIVER OF EMOTION

The quiver transforms the sound into music.

A feather caressing the mind,

Enters the bloodstream as feelings grow,

Becoming a current of emotions

That transform the soul into a celestial ship,

Carried by the current.

What begins as a quiver becomes a river;

The river becomes the ocean,

The ocean becomes an emotion,

And you feel it.

FORGOTTEN SOUNDS

GHAZAL OF LOVE

I cherish the fresh sounds of love;
Only the new can heal an old love.

As I watch the waves embrace the shore,
I long to be a wave of love.

In quarrels, there is no true hatred,
Only folly and a lack of love.

The sun shines upon me,
And I reflect that light upon the world with love.

I journey through my memories
To discover newfound love.

Sing to me, sea; sing to me, sky,
And let the world unfold from love.

A MAN WITH A GUITAR

Men talk in the public square,

Pigeons eat on the sidewalk and fly,

Women flirt and feed the pigeons.

Men, envious of pigeons,

Desire more attention from the women

But women only notice birds who know how to sing.

A nightingale starts singing

And attention moves from pigeons to nightingales;

There comes a man with a guitar, and he starts playing

And singing like a nightingale.

A woman allured by these new sounds

Forgets the pigeons and nightingales;

She shyly starts to sing

And turns to a man with a guitar.

THE BOOK OF BOOKS

An aspiring poet is usually advised
To use dictionaries, encyclopedias,
Grammar books, books of style, dictionary of rhyme,
Books on how to write and attendance at workshops.

To write, do write. But what about creativity?
How do you learn creativity? How to make sounds
Make love in the soul so one can continue
Making love with the page? How to

Learn from books that go unnoticed,
Gather glances, faces, metamorphoses
Of sounds, lives, territories, languages,
From a huge treasury of hidden sounds,

Hidden meanings flying in our faces unrecognized?
There is no grammar book to explain the world,
There is no book of style to explain the grace
Of a moonlight over the waves telling stories

To fishermen that learned from the sea;
To sailors, warriors that learned from losses and wins;
To birds that fly without support yet sing

Fed by notes from the biggest treasury

Of sounds, meanings, styles, dictionaries,
Histories, tragedies, deaths, births, revivals.
Yet this book is the place to start
And the place to go to for advice.

SERIOUS BUSINESS

If I were to share my struggles,
You might find it unsettling and discomforting
But there's no reason for that;
By sharing, we can start to recognize
The importance of simple beauty,
Which often goes ignored.

Busy with the expensive success,
We forget the free beauty—
Lying sad just around the corner,
Only an instant away,
Unnoticed and wasted.

SADNESS AND HAPPINESS

I cannot express everything I truly want to say,
And that makes me sad.

I cannot see all that I wish to see,
And that makes me sad.

I cannot visit even the closest neighbors in the Universe,
And that makes me sad.

I cannot read all that I want to read,
And that makes me sad.

I cannot love as much as I desire,
And that makes me sad.

I cannot be loved as much as I wish to be,
And that makes me sad.

But I have lived,
And for that, I am happy.

WISHFUL THINKING

"I wish I could sing like you,"
Said the frog to the nightingale.
"I would also like to have wings
So that I could fly while I sing,
Instead of having to jump from pond to pond."

"Caw, caw!" chirped the nightingale
As it flew away.

FERTILE GROUND

If raindrops

    D

    R

    O

    P

Into the right ears

    M

    U

    S

    I

    C

Starts growing from fertile ground

FORGOTTEN SOUNDS

No more messages,
No more instructions.
Stop!
Motors of progress,
Engines of alienation.

Forget
Big words and slogans,
Proclamations and declarations.

Wake up
To the forgotten sounds,
Sincere music.

Move
In a new direction,
From that very place.

Rediscover
The old melody
Of a sleepy world within you.
Then go,
Aiming as far as possible,
And never look back.

THE OLD SOUND

I am tired of all the new sounds;
They insult my sense of hearing.

I am weary of the countless variations of the same notes,
With this cacophony rearranged into new rhythms.

I can't hear anything anymore;
I feel like I am becoming deaf.

In a world filled with so many sounds,
I struggle to recognize any of them.

It's just a sea of noise—
Waves of sounds crashing monotonously.

Swimming in this ocean of indistinct noises,
I am unable to hear anything that brings me recognition.

I am frustrated and angry.

FORGOTTEN SERENADES

SERENADE

I enjoy serenading you,
Though I never admit it.
I serenade you when you can't hear anything
And while you are asleep.

I serenade you as you wake,
Never forgetting your preferences:
When you like it, and how you like it.
You enjoy waking up to calla lilies,

Along with my melodies,
And my plans for the new day,
You can hear the music when I invite you
To the park for lunch on a blanket.

You appreciate that I admire your jeans
As much as your gowns.
You enjoy that I understand you like
Grass as much as marble floors.

You cherish the sound of each morning
That brings new opportunities.
You value all the unseen gifts
That visually inspire you every day.

YOU ARE WHAT YOU SEE

They say *you are what you think,*
And they are right.
Your thoughts are shaped by what you see,
And they reflect your perceptions.

When you see the Light, you become the Light,
You transform into water that nurtures a flower,
A fountain flowing back into itself,
Opening up the entire Universe.

You perceive what you think,
And you become what you envision.
In the depths of your mind
You can foresee the Light ahead in the Darkness.

Your vision is your Light
Awakening you to the forgotten sound
Of the healer that sleeps within you.
That inner healer is your only Savior.

THE DRAMA OF LOVE AND HATE

Love and hate are driven by passion.
Both emotions originate from the heart
Entering our lives without much reasoning.
They can seem irrational, even dangerous—
Two opposing forces in the human experience.

The result is that hearts that harbor hate
Eventually corrode and lead to self-destruction,
While hearts that nourish love
Remain bright and serene,
Regardless of the circumstances.

There is hardly any remedy
For either a loving heart or a hating one.

A MAN AND HIS SHADOW

He walks down the street,
Followed by his shadow
As his only companion.
He asks the shadow for direction
Toward something new—
A new city, a new street,
A new life, new feelings.
He longs to escape his own skin
And follow a new shadow
Toward a new man,
New skin, new life.

"That is impossible,
I will always follow only you,"
The shadow replies.

END OF THE LABYRINTH

He tries to find the exit
Within himself,
But there is no door.

He walks
Through the inner labyrinth
To deceive his desires.

Perhaps there is an entrance
At the end of the labyrinth,
But there is no end.

MY OTHER SELF

I am a slave to desire,
I am a slave to pride,
I am a slave to vice,
I am a slave to success.

"Get rid of desire," desire said.
"Get rid of pride," pride said.
"Get rid of vices," honor said.
"Get rid of competition," success said.

I will still be a slave to sin,
A slave to materialism,
A slave to love,
A slave to myself.

"Get rid of sin and lust,
Of materialism and love,
And you will get rid of yourself,"
Said my other self.

"Are you proposing suicide?" I asked sadly.
"No, I would never suggest that," my other self replied.
"Then what are you trying to say?"
"Just be yourself," said my other self.

MY LIFE

My life made choices for me,
And many of them were poor;
My life endured hardships on my behalf,
And I felt their weight.

My life was both carefree and strict;
I was its disciple.
My life embraced joy for me,
And I felt it within.

This could easily become a very long list,
One that may never end;
I must cut it short,
And my life senses it.

THE LAND BEYOND

There is a land beyond our land,
There is life beyond our lives,
There is a world we do not see.
It seems to be beyond far
Because it's far within and near.

The world beyond and the world here,
Both worlds are far and near.
The farthest land is also the closest.
It's not a matter of time and space,
It is a matter of sense and attitude—

To know how to stay in yet fly far,
To understand how to stay outside
When moving far in what is near.

KNOWLEDGE

If we had true insight,
We would be terrified.
We could see nothing,
Yet perceive everything and nothing at once.

Our senses highlight our limitations.
They expand our vision within certain boundaries
And enhance our understanding through pleasure.
Without pleasure, there is no sight nor measure.

Complete knowledge leads to the annihilation
Of the desire to see, touch, or feel.
The world is experienced only through our senses
And remains untouched by knowledge alone, without feeling.

OLD AND NEW

If an ancient man had seen planes two thousand years ago
He would have thought they were birds
Or angels from another world
Or messengers from other planets.

Every new machine would have surprised him—
The car, the TV, the radio, the phone, the camera.
He might have believed he was a savage
Who didn't understand these marvels.

If he had seen a computer
And observed people talking on the Internet,
He would have thought it was a civilization
Much more advanced than his own.

After spending time among these messengers,
He would have learned that every child possessed
Knowledge and understanding of these technologies,
And knew how to use them.

Yet, after a while, he would have noticed
That none of them were advanced enough
To be considered wiser than the one
Who stated, "I know nothing."

PEOPLE

Some people complain there are too many people on earth,
Some people complain about secret societies,
Some people accuse others of not being able to wake up early,
Almost all people complain about something.

No people get rid of themselves to solve problem No.1,
No people disclose their agendas to solve problem No.2,
No people learn how to discipline themselves to solve problem
   No.3,
All people are enslaved by something.

FAITH

From dust to dust,
From ashes to ashes.
Is that all there is?

DICTIONARY OF SOUNDS

DICTIONARY OF SOUNDS

Born from the natural attraction
Of vowels and consonants
Alliterating or merging into a fugue

Of sounds flowing
From the fountain of language.
Meanings embodied

In blasts of thunder, chirping, blowing;
Sounds becoming meanings
In, for, and of themselves;

A huge dictionary of sounds
Craving to be recognized and translated
Either into language or into understanding.

ECHO

When you hear an idea
Lying between the sounds and the letters,
You uncover its meaning.

A sound flows silently
In the Universe, waiting
To be discovered in the obvious.

The Universe smiles,
Or you may find an omen
In a hostile land of the unknown.

Dig deeper and work harder;
Grow in the opposite direction
To see what lies beneath.

This effort nourishes the surface of sounds,
Allowing you to witness their creation
And hear their echoes on the way back home.

SOUND BOMBS

Everything in nature exists
Based on the law of attraction.
Lovemaking derives from that law,
Fighting comes from the friction of conquest.

We can be scared by sounds
Or seduced by sounds;
Sounds can kill us
Or reach heavenly heights.

Nobody has yet conceived a Sound Bomb—
Stronger than nuclear or neutron bombs.
It would be a fantastic bomb.
It could be the first bomb tested in outer space;

It could be sent far to distract
The future asteroid ready to strike the Earth;
It could be sent as a signal
To other civilizations throughout the Universe.

We should be careful with sound ideas,
For anyone may exploit them
And split the planet in half
While testing some new Sound.

EMISSARIES

Timeo Danaos et dona ferentes

They will come again with offerings,
Smiling as they always do
When planning a major attack
Late at night.

Be aware of the high notes,
Blissful faces, and their soft messages.
Listen for the silent sound
Of a finely wrapped gift.

PARADISE

Noise is needed for attention,
Flashy disposable sounds
Flushed after one use

To seduce and amuse sleepy spirits
With another sound, another appearance
Of an elevated spirit waiting

To come out into the big world
Ready for a new spectacle
A new Genie from a bottle

Of dreams sold in big boxes
Waving from the shelves,
Waving from billboards,

From the TV and the radio waves
Ready to come out,
Inviting us into a paradise
Decorated with Hell.

TODAY AND TOMORROW

There is always tomorrow,

Sounds of hope smiling from the distance

Alluring, drawing us into unknown territory;

There is always hope

We will arrive safely into the future,

Experience an unavoidable arrival of time waiting;

There is always time on hold,

To cut the future waiting

For those in the present time;

There is also sorrow

That doesn't wait for tomorrow.

TWO SOUNDS TALKING

Silence: I am a silent sound.
Sound: I am a sound sound.

Sound: Can I hear you if you are silent?
Silence: Yes you can, if you listen to me.

Sound: How can I listen to you if you are silent?
Silence: That is the whole point.

Sound: What is the whole point?
Silence: To learn how to listen to me.

Sound: If I learn, will I really hear you?
Silence: Yes, you will.

Sound: And you will sound like a sound?
Silence: I will sound like thunder.

Sound: That is nonsense—I am thunder.
Silence: Yes, a thunder of silence.

Silence: Who have you been talking to all this time?
Sound: You.

Silence: Who else could hear you without me?

Sound: Nobody.

Silence: There can be no sound without silence.

I am the Mother of all sounds.

Sound: You're right, Mother. You gave us life

And we all return to you either in quiet or with thunder.

SOUNDS OF LIFE AND LOVE

Love: Which is more important: Love or life?
Life: Without life, there would be no love.

Love: But without love, life would have no meaning.
Life: True, but life gives birth to love.

Love: And what gives rise to life?
Life: Life generates itself.

Love: Nothing can give birth to itself automatically,
There must be some cause, reason, or action.

Life: Life exists without any cause.
Love: If life is without a cause, then it lacks purpose.

Life: The purpose of life is to live.
Love: No, the purpose of life is love.

Life: You must be born to exist.
Without life, there is nothing.

Love: Life is nothing unless it comes from an inherent love.
You just don't understand.

SOUNDS OF LOVE AND HATE

Shall I say I love you? says Love.

No, you shall not.

Love loses its magic when declared.

Also, you would not be Love if you did not love me,

Says Hate.

Shall I say I hate you? says Hate.

No, you shall not.

I already know you hate me.

You would not be hate if you didn't hate me,

Says Love.

But if I said I hate you, what would you do? asks Love.

I would not believe you, says Hate.

Then I must kill you, says Love.

Then, you will be lonely, says Hate

And you will not be Love anymore.

You would kill yourself and become me.

FUTURE MAN

Perhaps you will laugh at me now,
But I forgive you.
I am already laughing
Along with you.

BEAUTY NEVER DIES

INVISIBLE TEACHER

You guide us on what to do,
Yet you often abandon us in critical moments,
Leaving us to fight alone.

You help us learn to walk,
But in times of isolation,
You leave us to rely on ourselves.

We stumble over obstacles
And though you are a teacher,
You are never a source of immediate help.

You are rarely warm enough—almost indifferent—
As you watch shipwrecks and broken homes,
Always unflinching.

You teach us in advance,
But remain silent when we need you most.
Your whereabouts are always unknown to us.

THE MOST IMPORTANT THINGS

The most important things are often unspoken—
Meaningful truths that surround us.
Unmerited treasures greet us at every turn—
Beauty unseen, waiting for a curious gaze,
Not too busy to notice the obvious.

You travel and breathe deeply,
Speechless yet aware of the unexpressed.
You search for the key to significant words,
And for a long time, you wait alone
To hear them emerge from the silence.

BEAUTY NEVER DIES

Singers may pass, but a song never dies,
Feeding the eternal flame.

New minds ignite,
Eager eyes yearn to listen, kindling passion.

Beauty recognizes the spark,
Shyly seducing from afar.

Beauty nurtures the flame,
Eyes cherish the beauty.

The source of fire—an omnipotent eye—
Hearing with eyes, seeing with ears.

THE LIFE OF WORDS

Some words fade away from too much freedom,
While others exist under oppression.
Some words expand in meaning,
While others merely reproduce.

Words that flourish through expression survive
And gain value and freedom,
But those that are forcefully multiplied
Diminish in worth, consumed by other words.

A FIFTY-FIFTY GAME

Suddenly, everything changed,

And nothing seemed as clear anymore—

At least, that's how it felt.

We don't know whom to blame now:

Deceiving eyes and misleading knowledge

Or God and a world guilty of trickery?

Are we betting on what our eyes see,

Or on what the world conceals?

It seems to be a fifty-fifty game.

APPEARANCES

We believed we had unraveled the mystery,
Convinced we understood the world,
Yet, nothing is more powerful than change,
Nothing is more healing or sobering,
Nothing else opens our eyes wider,
Making everything seem different.

A MORE IMPORTANT WORLD

There is a deeper world within you,
Waiting to be discovered—
Something profound yet unseen.
You can sense it on the sandy beach
As you listen to the tireless waves;
You hear a forgotten story.
Or, when lying on the grass,
You become one with the soil.
You can feel it beneath the oak tree
As you follow its shadow,
More precise than a Swiss watch,
You hear the clock inside you,
Suddenly awakening you.

SELF-RESPECT

Wherever you go,
You will always be yourself.

You may feel the urge to run away quickly:
That's how we learn to forget.

This strategy involves keeping yourself busy
And making it part of your daily routine.

It may be effective if your goal is to forget,
But if you wish to confront your feelings,
You must face them directly.

OBLIVION

To be born, to be young, to grow old, and to die—
To burn, to fly, to scream, to love, to live, and to die for life.

Without the ability to walk and feel tired,
What would you be?

But without understanding, why go through all of this—
Are you, or are you not?

What would you do to forget if, by chance,
You found what you were searching for?

What would you do, and would you regret
Ever asking the question, "Why?"

Eternal peace will handle everything,
And you will fall into oblivion without being asked.

LIFE AND TIME

Life and time are inseparable.
Without one, there is no other.
The vigor of life tells the story of time.

Time is a human construct—
A broken clock.

ABOUT THE AUTHOR

Dejan Stojanović (1959) was born in Peć, Kosovo (formerly part of Serbia, Yugoslavia). Although he received a legal education, he has never practiced law. Instead, he became a journalist and foreign correspondent in the early 1990s; however, he is primarily a poet, essayist, philosopher, and businessman.

He has published the following poetry collections:

Circling (Krugovanje), Narodna knjiga—Alfa, Belgrade, published in three editions: 1993, 1998, and 2000.
The Sun Watches Itself (Sunce sebe gleda), NIP Književna reč, Belgrade, 1999.
The Sign and Its Children (Znak i njegova deca), Prosveta, Belgrade, 2000.
The Creator (Tvoritelj), Narodna knjiga, Belgrade, 2000.
The Shape (Oblik), Gramatik, Podgorica, 2000.

The Dance of Time (Ples vremena), Konras, Belgrade, 2007.

Pentalogy: *The World in Nowherness (Svet u nigdini),* Udruženje književnika Srbije, Belgrade, 2017:
(1) *Ozar (Ozar),*
(2) *The World and God (Svet i Bog),*
(3) *The World in Nowhereness (Svet u nigdini),*
(4) *The World and Humans (Svet i ljudi),*
(5) *The Home of Light (Dom svetlosti).*

The Hidden Light (Skrivena svetlost), Čigoja, Belgrade, 2018.
Primordial Spark (Iskra iskona), Albatros plus, Belgrade, 2021.
Centuries and Steps (Vekovi i koraci), Albatros plus, Belgrade, 2023.

Essays:
Creator and Creating (Stvaralac i stvaranje), Albatros plus, Belgrade, 2021.
The New Man and the New World (Novočovek i novosvet), Rad, Belgrade, 2022.

Anthology: *Selected Serbian Plays* (*Izabrane srpske drame*), USA, 2016.

A book of his selected interviews, *Conversations* (*Razgovori*), was published in 1999 by NIP Književna reč in Belgrade. The Serbian Heritage Foundation and the Association of Writers of Serbia for Intellectual Engagement awarded the book the Rastko Petrović Prize.

Collected Poems: 1978-2000 (Pentalogy 1), New Avenue Books, 2025 (Translation from Serbian).

Books written in English:

Philosophy: *Absolute,* New Avenue Books, USA, 2024.

Poetry Series: *The Embrace of Light and Darkness* (Pentalogy 3):
- *Dance of Sounds*, New Avenue Books, 2025
- *The Matter of Matter*, New Avenue Books, 2025
- *The Home of the World*, New Avenue Books, 2025
- *All Women in One*, New Avenue Books, 2025
- *Strange Thoughts* (prose), New Avenue Books, 2025

He lived in Chicago, USA, from 1990 to 2014, and holds citizenship in both Serbia and the United States.

www.ingramcontent.com/pod-product-compliance
Lightning Source LLC
Chambersburg PA
CBHW052014240626
47153CB00008B/2874